This Topsy and Tim book belongs to

_____

This title was previously published as part of the *Topsy and Tim Learnabout* series
Published by Ladybird Books Ltd
80 Strand London WC2R ORL
A Penguin Company

7 9 10 8 6

© Jean and Gareth Adamson MCMXCV

This edition MMIII

ISBN-13: 978-1-90435-121-4
ISBN-10: 1-90435-121-2

Printed in Italy

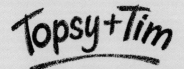

Topsy+Tim

Go to the Zoo

Jean and **Gareth Adamson**

Topsy and Tim were going to the zoo.
First they made sure their pets had all they
needed for their day at home.
"Let's ask the zoo animals if they would like
to come home with us," said Topsy.
"Animals can't answer questions!" said Tim.

Topsy and Tim met the penguins first.
They walked like funny old men but
they dived and swam beautifully.

Topsy and Tim would
have liked the penguins
to come home with them
but they looked so happy
in the zoo.

The parrots in the aviary were making
a dreadful noise. Topsy had heard that
parrots could answer questions, so she
asked one, "Would you like to come
home with us?"

"Ripe bananas, brown bread,"
squawked the parrot.

"I'm afraid parrots don't give sensible
answers," said Dad.

They took a ride on the elephant's back.

"We're the highest in the whole zoo," said Tim.

Then they saw a giraffe. She was higher still, although her feet were on the ground.

"Look!" said Tim.
"Horses in football jerseys."
The zebras showed how they could kick.
One kicked another with his back hooves.
"We don't want those zebras at home," said Dad.
"They might kick us."

"Look! White teddy bears!" said Topsy.

"Those are polar bears," said Mummy,
"and they are very fierce."
"We won't take them home," said Tim.

A crowd of people hurried past Topsy and Tim.

"They are going to watch the lions being fed," said Mummy.

"Let's go too!" shouted Topsy and Tim.

The keeper brought huge lumps
of meat for the lions.

It was fun to see them enjoying their food.

Topsy and Tim were hungry.
Mummy found a slot-machine that
sold orange drinks and chocolate.
Topsy and Tim thought it was a
good slot-machine.

The sea-lions were hungry too.
The keeper threw them fish
from a bucket.

"Can we take a sea-lion home?"
asked Tim.
"No," said Topsy.
"It might eat our goldfish."

Topsy and Tim wanted to take all the monkeys home. But it was time for Mummy and Dad to take Topsy and Tim home.

Topsy and Tim were glad they had not brought any zoo animals home. Their own pet animals were just as interesting and they were good old friends too.

"I don't know why we go to the zoo," said Dad. "We've got our own zoo at home."